Dear Parent:
Your child's love of reading starts here!

Every child learns to read in a different way and at his or her own speed. Some go back and forth between reading levels and read favorite books again and again. Others read through each level in order. You can help your young reader improve and become more confident by encouraging his or her own interests and abilities. From books your child reads with you to the first books he or she reads alone, there are I Can Read Books for every stage of reading:

SHARED READING
Basic language, word repetition, and whimsical illustrations, ideal for sharing with your emergent reader

BEGINNING READING
Short sentences, familiar words, and simple concepts for children eager to read on their own

READING WITH HELP
Engaging stories, longer sentences, and language play for developing readers

READING ALONE
Complex plots, challenging vocabulary, and high-interest topics for the independent reader

ADVANCED READING
Short paragraphs, chapters, and exciting themes for the perfect bridge to chapter books

I Can Read Books have introduced children to the joy of reading since 1957. Featuring award-winning authors and illustrators and a fabulous cast of beloved characters, I Can Read Books set the standard for beginning readers.

A lifetime of discovery begins with the magical words "I Can Read!"

Visit www.icanread.com for information
on enriching your child's reading experience.

To Spike
—R.S.

I Can Read Book® is a trademark of HarperCollins Publishers.

Splat the Cat: Good Night, Sleep Tight Copyright © 2011 by Rob Scotton All rights reserved. Printed in the United States of America. No part of this book may be used or reproduced in any manner whatsoever without written permission except in the case of brief quotations embodied in critical articles and reviews. For information address HarperCollins Children's Books, a division of HarperCollins Publishers, 10 East 53rd Street, New York, NY 10022.
www.icanread.com

Library of Congress Cataloging-in-Publication Data
Scotton, Rob.
    Good night, sleep tight / based on the bestselling books by Rob Scotton ; cover art by Rob Scotton ; interior illustrations by Robert Eberz.—1st ed.
       p.   cm.
    Summary: Splat is excited about camping out until his mother surprises him with the news that Spike and Plank will be there, too.
    ISBN 978-0-06-197856-2 (trade bdg.) —ISBN 978-0-06-197855-5 (pbk.)
    [1. Camping—Fiction.   2. Cats—Fiction.] 1. Title.
PZ7.G60138   2011   2010027753
[E] 22   CIP
                                                                                                                                AC

            11   12   13   14   15   LP/WOR   10   9   8   7   6   5   4   3   2   ❖   First Edition

I Can Read!

BEGINNING
1
READING

Splat the Cat
Good Night, Sleep Tight

Based on the bestselling books
by Rob Scotton

Cover art by Rob Scotton

Text by Natalie Engel

Interior illustrations by Robert Eberz

HARPER

An Imprint of HarperCollins Publishers

Splat was happy.

It was almost night.

He was getting ready

to camp under the moonlight!

"Everything is just right,"

Splat told his mom.

"I have my sleeping bag.

I have my flashlight."

"And I have a surprise,"
said Splat's mom.
"Let's go outside."

Mom and Splat

went into the garden.

They pulled back the tent flaps.

Splat peered inside the tent.

Two sets of eyes peered back.

"Say hello to Spike and Plank,"

said Splat's mom.

"They are camping here tonight!"

Splat felt his whiskers

wobble with fright.

"Mom," whispered Splat,

"I don't like Spike."

"You might like him better

if you spent some time together,"

said Splat's mom.

"You'll see.

Everything will be just right."

"I'm hungry," said Spike.

"What did you bring

for me to eat?"

"I have some fish cakes,"

Splat said.

"Yum," said Spike.

He gobbled them up in delight.

"Look," said Splat.

"The stars are so bright.

I see at least a million."

"I see seventy-one," said Plank.

"I see nothing," said Spike,

"but two silly cats

looking at the moonlight."

"It's getting late," said Splat.

"Let's try to sleep."

But Plank could not rest.

"My sleeping bag

is much too tight," he said.

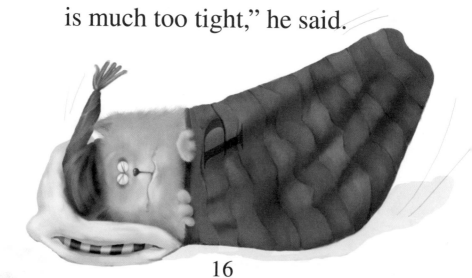

Plank tossed. He turned.

He struggled, stretched, and strained.

RRRIP!

"You're welcome," said Spike.

Splat was just about to fall asleep

when something felt wrong.

He saw a dark shadow

creep up the tent wall.

"Run for your lives!"

Splat shouted

with all his might.

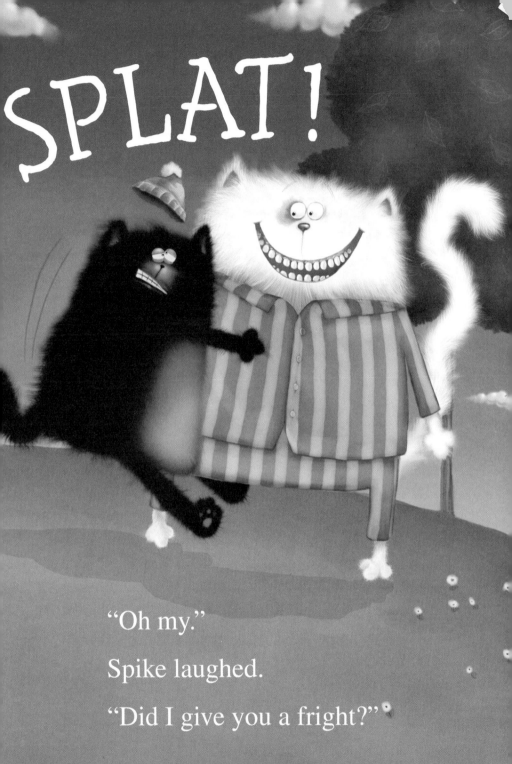

SPLAT!

"Oh my."

Spike laughed.

"Did I give you a fright?"

"What's the big deal?" said Spike.

"Everything is all right."

Splat did not think so.

But he was too tired

to pick a fight.

One by one,

Splat's whiskers drooped.

One by one,

his eyes shut tight.

Suddenly, Spike sprang up.

"What's wrong?" said Splat.

"There's something strange

crawling up my leg!" yelled Spike.

"Mommy!" screamed Spike.

He scrambled out of his sleeping bag.

He stumbled out of the tent.

When Spike took flight,

he took the whole tent

down with him.

"Oh, Seymour!" said Splat.

"It was just you."

"It's all right, Spike!

Come back!" said Splat and Plank.

"We will protect each other

for the rest of the night."

"Promise?" sniffled Spike.

"Promise," said Splat.

"Now good night," said Splat.

"Sleep tight," said Plank.

"See you in the morning light," said Spike.

31

For three friends

who camped out that night,

everything turned out just right.